YUSUF AND ZULEKHA

A STORY OF YUSUF (A.S)

QASIM KASHMIRI

Made with ♥ on the Notion Press Platform
www.notionpress.com

To all my Readers

Contents

PREFACE

<u>About the author</u>

Qasim Kashmiri is a Poet and Novelist from north Kashmir Baramlla. He has authored the books like "Secret Of Dark Nights, The Ashes, and Colour Of My Bones. He is masters in English literature and working as a teacher. He has been writing since 2017 and continue to write about the diverse topics from poetry to fiction. He is deeply influenced by the works of Moulana Rumi. Yusuf and Zulekha is his first book that is concerned about religious importance and first book that is based on the story of Prophet Yusuf and his hardships he had gone through till he became the king of Egypt.

PROLOGUE

About The Book

The book 'Yusuf and zulekha is a life lesson story Prophet Yusuf (a.s) which is detailed in twelfth chapter in the Quran with a name sura Yusuf. This book is originally the commentary about the story of Yusuf how he dreamed about his father, mother and step brothers and asked his father Yaqoob for the interpretations. This also mentions how the step brothers cast him into the well and later Yusuf was sold in Egypt and was brought up the house of Aziz and Zulekha and spent his most years in the prison for wrong allegations. This book is written with the references taken from the different tafaseer like, bayan ul Quran by Dr Asrar a.r, Tafeemul Quran by Moulana Moududi r.a and Ibne Qaseer. There is nothing written by the author of his own accord and the book is not based on fictional sources. The book is divided into chapters that give it the finest form to be read in the form one complete book form the beginning to end.

I

Chapter

One day Yusuf (a.s) whispered to his father, prophet Yaqoob (a.s), "dear Abba, I had a dream in which I saw eleven stars, the moon and the sun, after a pause he continued with hesitation, I saw them prostrating before me". It was the time when Yusuf was just a kid. When Yaqoob came to know about Yusuf's dream, he replied, "do not reveal this dream to your elder brothers, maybe they would plot a conspiracy against you, certainly Satan is the exposed enemy of the man". Yaqoob understood that my son has been blessed by Allah to confer him with the prophet-hood. Yaqub knew that Allah will bless Yusuf with full understanding of the problems of life and their solutions; he will give him insight to reach at the reality of every matter.

The interpretation of the dream was quite obvious; Yaqub had a genuine fear that Yusuf's ten step brothers would become all more envious of him when they would hear this. He warned Yusuf not to mention his dream to his brothers, he knew his sons will not bear the moral character of Yusuf and they would end up to any evil design to him out of mere envy. Yaqub knew his ten sons are not of right type, it was proved by the subsequent events and Yaqub was not happy with them.As regards to the dream, the son in it was Yaqub, the "moon" his wife (Yusuf's mother), and the "eleven stars" his eleven brothers.

Yaqoob had two wives, an elderly wife had got ten sons, who had attained the age of maturity and from the second wife of Yaqoob they had got two sons, Yusuf and bin-yamin. Bin-yamin was the real younger brother of Yusuf who was of his junior by many years. The Quran has not mentioned the name of any wife of Yaqoob.

All the step brothers of Yusuf said that our father likes Yusuf more than us, he is very beloved to Abba even though we are grown-ups and sturdier than him. Our father surely is doing wrong, they added.They remarked, " our father seems to have lost his balance of mind, otherwise he could not have neglected us and loved our two younger brothers more than us, we are strong young men and can stand him in good stead at the time of need while these youngsters are useless, as they themselves need protection"."We will kill Yusuf or throw him away far from the father", they plotted. All the step brothers were not willing to kill or hurt by any means to Yusuf but their lust and their wicked intentions encouraged them to do it. They decided to kill him or take him away from his father so that all the attention of Yaqoob would turn to them. They hoped that after committing such sin and doing such a wicked thing to Yusuf , they will still remain with one of those who do right, they hoped to remain God fearing even in the full knowledge of their actions were wrong. They lacked the power of reason and the character of true believer.

One of the brothers whose name was Yehuda who was also the eldest and kind one said to other nine ones, "if you really want to kill him, don't kill but take him away and throw in some well far from the home, maybe some caravan from anywhere would take him along". In that times there used to be the biggest wells on the way sides which used to be very narrow, dark with open mouth. Those wells often found on the ways where all the caravans would travel and drink water and pass by.

The rest of the nine brothers were convinced to accept the idea of their elder brother, he could not succeed to change their filthy intrigue but finally convinced them to throw him in the well which at least can save the life of Yusuf and he could be alive if some caravan will find and take him along.

All the step brothers of Yusuf asked their father, 'Abba, we assume you don't trust us with regard to Yusuf even though we are his well-wishers'.Why you don't allow us to take Yusuf along with us for the sports so he can grow up with some knowledge of playing and grow the way we did', they added.They said, ' let Yusuf come with us tomorrow for the hunting, he will take interest in sport and eat fruits from the trees around and you should not worry about him , we are his protectors and we will surely take care of him.'It Troubles me that you should take him away with you, if you take him and you will be eventful in the sports meanwhile some wolf would come to eat him up', replied Yaqoob.

They replied back, 'if a wolf should eat him up in our company even we are a band then we are worthless people indeed'. They tried to convince their father that Yusuf is their brother as all the other ten brothers who are too dear to each other.After persisting like this, they took him along with them, and decided to cast them away into the dark well

And one day they took Yusuf along and did the same thing that they intended to do. When they cast Yusuf into the well. There Allah revealed to Yusuf that a time will come when you will admonish them about this action they did, now they do not comprehend its consequences.At night fall they returned to their father, weeping, wailing and said, 'O Abba, we were observed in running races and we had left Yusuf with our things when a wolf came and devoured him but you will never believe us even though if we are truthful and for the proof they brought his shirt with false blood upon it.Hearing this Yqaqoob said; your evil souls had made this easy for you, what I can do is to be patient and Allah will reveal what you did.

The behaviour of Yusuf's brothers confirmed the correctness of their doubts that their father felt about them. The fact they coming weeping was the clear sigh of ruthlessness of their behaviour. They tried to make other people feel sorry for them and portrayed themselves helpless.

After some time, a caravan passed by that well. They sent their water carrier, a man who used to walk in front of caravan and lead it as well. A man put a bucket into the well for lilting the water, seeing Yusuf in the well he cried, 'good news! Here is a young lad, the caravan took him away from the well and hid him as merchandise, they decided to sell him away and have some money. The caravan recued Yusuf though they would be able to sell him and regarded him as a piece of merchandise.

The caravan sold Yusuf for a few dirhams which were the least price; they sold him to have money, because of the system of slavery in Egypt and surrounding. People actively engaged in a trade, buying and selling children in particular. They had no idea who actually that lad (Yusuf) was. They had no attention to keep him with them as they considered Yusuf just boy to be raised up as a slave.

In Egypt the man who bought Yusuf who was at prime position in the Egyptian govt, his name was Al-Aziz (Aziz Miser). When he brought Yusuf home, he told his wife,' take good care of this boy, maybe he can prove to be useful to us and later we may adopt him. They decided to raise him up as their son and teach him the affairs of govt. This is how Yusuf was taken from well and reached to royal family; Allah had best plans for him which his brother could not understand.

Al-Aziz had a very high opinion of Yusuf from the very beginning. He came to conclusion that he belonged to some noble family and had been made a slave by force of adverse circumstances. When Yusuf was taken to Aziz, he said, "he doesn't look like a slave and I fear he has been stolen from his country and his home that's why Aziz did not treat him like a slave and put him in charge of his house and possessions.Though Yusuf reached the place of most cultured and civilised countries of the known world, where he required a different experience and training for conduct of its affairs. Allah made all arrangements for this, sent him to the house of an officer of very high rank in Egypt, who entrusted him with full powers of his house and estate.

II
Chapter

Yusuf stepped into his maturity and grew young with elegance; Allah gave him wisdom and knowledge. The knowledge he started to attain was the revelation by Allah to him.

The lady of the house where Yusuf lived in wanted to seduce him. Her name was zulekha and she was the wife of Aziz. Zulekha began to tempt him and started to invite him for evil. One day she closed the doors of her house and said to Yusuf, 'come here'. A suitable environment was prepared to that end. Yusuf replied, 'may Allah protect me how can I be so bad to perform this act?"How can I be among the unfaithful to my lord, who gave me shelter and everything? My lord has shown much kindness to me, should I then misbehave like this"?This was the divine argument that saved Yusuf from the great temptation. Even though he was in in his youth.

Yusuf feared Allah and prayed to over of the deception. He was pious to even he could not think of it for a moment. He avoided transgressing and tried to escape from the woman.Zulekha slandered him despite of his virtuous behaviour and avoidance of sin but Yusuf rushed towards the closed door.She chased him till the door and rent his shirt from behind. Yusuf opened the door. While opening the door both Yusuf and zulekha found Aziz approaching towards them.Seeing her husband at the door she cried out'"What punishments does one deserve who shows evil intentions towards your wife?"'What else than this that he should be put in the prison or tormented with painful torment' she added. She told her husband that he had approached her with evil intentions, demanding that he either be put in prison or suffer torture".Yusuf stood still and said, 'it was she who implored me'.

Meanwhile a man from her relation reached the circumstances. He asked to check Yusuf's shirt, if it is torn from the back then zulekha would be guilty and if the shirt is found torn from the front then Yusuf will be sentenced to imprisonment or tormented for his evil intentions. Therefore the judgments were made over the shirt of Yusuf from the both sides. The man who made this decision on judging the situation was truthful man though he was related to zulekha and Aziz.

After the arguments when Aziz found the shirt was torn from the back he said,' indeed this is one of the traps of women; your traps are indeed strange'.Finding his wife guilty he said to Yusuf, "Yusuf, forget about this accident and turning to his wife he added,' "you are indeed the one who had evil intentions for that you must repent before Allah". Yet the incident did not end there, it went up to another horizons.

Time passed by and the matter spread out in the whole city. Everyone started taking about Yusuf and zulekha. The women in the vicinity deeply took curiosity in the matter and all of them begun to stretch this like something very strange. It became the house hold talk and especially women of the town began murmuring that the wife of Aziz has been soliciting her slave, for she has passionately fallen in love with him. We think that she transparently is doing a wrong thing.

Zulekha came across the issue that the women in the town begun to speak against Zulekha and her wicked conduct with her slave, condemning her actions. When zulekha realised that she had become the target of gossiping, she prepared a trap for them. To answering all these women of the high rank officials; she decided to serve them some party and decided to invite them for a feast. The aim to invite them was to show that she was not entirely to be blamed for succumbing to her immoral urges with respect to Yusuf because he was such an extraordinary beautiful man that every woman can amaze on his beauty.

Zulekha knew that the wives in her city are not polite if they also can be taken into matter of immoral, she knew all the women in the neighbourhood as well as their activities they do.She invited all these women to bouquet at her house, the women seated and rested their backs on pillows, ancient Egyptians used to place pillows and cautions in such feasts for the guests to recline. Slaves served them some fruits to eat with the knives. The entire women started to eat the fruits, cutting with knives.

Suddenly Zulekha gestured Yusuf to enter the ballroom where all ladies were seated. When Yusuf entered the room, all at once exclaimed, "Oh this is not a man, he is some noble angel"! They got bewildered but seeing Yusuf in front of them, they cut their fingers in wonder. They lost their senses in astonishment; they could not resist their emotions and hurt their hands.

Zulekha perceived the situation and announced with pride," well this is he whom you blamed me for, no doubt I sought to seduce him but he escaped, yet if he does not do what I want, he surely would be send to prison". She actually wanted let those women realise that if they had slave like Yusuf they would have done the same with him.Zulekha warned Yusuf in front these women; she again invited Yusuf for evil and warned if he doesn't it he surely shall be cast into prison and shall be humble and disgraced.

This open demonstration of love and declaration of her moral design shows the moral conditions of higher class of Egyptian society. This society had lowered to least moral values. The ladies that Zulekha invited also belonged to higher ranked society of the city.

In response to zulekha, Yusuf turned to Allah and prayed, "O Allah I prefer imprisonment to which to she invite me to. I seek help from you to protect me from her traps, if you don't save me, I might fall in this evil and counted with ignorant".Allah granted his prayed and saved him from the traps of these women.Undoubtedly, zulekha had madly fallen in love with Yusuf, after this accident the fame of Yusuf's beauty spread all over the country and other ladies of the capital came to know about him. It was the time when Yusuf was no more hidden name in the capital, through these temptations and tests, he came the house hold name and hi character turned as clear as a sheet of water.

Later, Yusuf was set into prison. The women and the all officials of the state were well acquainted about the character of Yusuf. They knew that Yusuf is man of honour and out beyond the values of the common man, but despite this familiarly of Yusuf they still sent him to prison.Till the time everyone in the Egypt had come to know about

Yusuf , he had become the biggest noun in the city and his character has put a heavy mark on every one of mind , sending him to prison actually qualified him the virtuous man and indeed he was.Yusuf surely was sent to prison without any guilt, it also manifested that the kingdom in the capital that time was full of lie and based of false foundations. His all allegations were baseless and he was innocent as crystal clear. Incidentally, an imprisonment of Yusuf without any trial and due procedure of law was the proof of filthy civilization itself. Egyptian rulers were honest to their dishonesty; they imprisoned Yusuf to safeguard their own interests.

III

Chapter

When Yusuf was in the prison. His age was around 21 years. There were other two slaves (men) in the prison who accompanied Yusuf in the same prison. Both of them were imprisoned because of their culpability, the drink server of the king, one day there found a fly in a drink and the stone grifts in a bread during the feast by the king and for that they too were cast into the prison.

The cellmates of Yusuf realised that he is not an ordinary man and alike the all prisoners around. They began to give him regard and respect as they had believed him to be the honourable man. They were deeply impressed by the elegance of Yusuf the things Yusuf believed in Allah. Yusuf spoke to them and talked about his forefathers and their character, he let them know that he believes in Allah alone and worship only him.

One day both the prison-mates came to Yusuf and revealed their dreams to him for interpretation. One prisoner said, 'I dreamed that I am pressing grapes into wine and the other said, "I dreamed that I am carrying loaves of bread on my head, of which birds are eating". Then both of them said, "Tell us their interpretations for we have seen that you are the righteous man.Both the prisoners whispered that we found you different from the rest of the prisoners and your character is different and exemplary among the all.Yusuf replied," I will tell you an interpretations of your dreams before the food you get comes to you. Yusuf made them calm about their dreams he said not to worry and convinced tom tell them the perfect interpretations."This ability of making interpretations that I am going to tell you is the part of knowledge that Allah had bestowed me, that fact is that I do not follow the ways of those who do not believe in Allah " Yusuf elaborated.

Yusuf also added in his words and said, "I am following the ways of my forefathers, Abrahim, Ishaaq and Yaqoob (as). It is not possible for us to associate the partners with Allah. This is the blessing of Allah that he had not made us slaves of anyone but himself". My fellow prisoners, here is the interpretations of your dreams," one of you will serve wine to his lord (king of Egypt) and for the other one he shall be crucified and the birds will eat up his head".

Since one of them got back to his earlier position to serve drinks to his lord and other prisoner was sentenced to death. Yusuf told to the one who was taken back to his service that tell your lord that there is one more innocent prisoner (Yusuf) in the cell and he was supposed to release him.But it was unfortunate that the man forgot to mention Yusuf to his lord (king) for which Yusuf spent several years in the prison.

Yusuf knew that was the most adventurous outcome, this was actually a test for patience and there is no doubt that spending many years in prison and forgetting is hard for most people. Yusuf confirmed the supremacy of his moral values and faith, greeted everything that happened to him with submission to will of Allah.

The king who ruled Egypt was from the Hyksos dynasty. One day the king himself dreamed and could not interpret his dream; he seemed to be confused and could not understand the meaning of the dream. For the interpretation of his own dream he called up his courtiers and said,' I saw a dream in which I saw seven fat cows devouring seven lean cows and seven green ears of corn and seven withered ones, tell me the interpretation of my dream if you understand their meaning'.

The courtiers answered, 'these are the results of confused nightmares, and we do not understand their meaning'. None of his courtiers could interpret; they too seemed confused as their lord (king).One of the two prisoners who was taken back to serve drinks to the king remembered Yusuf when the king wanted the interpretation of his dream. He said, "I know someone in the prison who flawlessly interpret the dreams and asked the king to send him to prison to ask Yusuf about the dream. "He has deep knowledge of interpreting the dreams "the man addedFinally the man convinced his lord and entered the cell to meet Yusuf for the interpretation of a dream.

When the man entered the prison and said to Yusuf, "the king has dreamed that the seven fat cows are eating up the seven lean cows and the seven green ears of corn and seven withered ones, now the king seems to be chaotic and do not understand the meaning of the dream , he wanted to interpret the dream".

Yusuf started to interpret the dream and announced," you will cultivate land for seven consecutive years as usual, during this period thrush out the harvest that you reap only that much grain that might suffice the need and store the rest of it. Then, after this there will be seven hard (drought) years upon you, then you will eat up all that corn that you might have kept for that period except that you would have reserved in the store. After that will come another year in which there will be abundant rainfall which will be very productive upon you, people will grow massive amount of grapes".

Yusuf did not only interpret the dream but he also suggested certain ways how to deal with these years when they come. He beautifully explained how seven years in the country will pass through contentment and the other seven years will be the years of drought when the realm will face the challenges of food scarcity and all. The ways he suggested would never have been in the mind of that kingdom.

He interpreted the dream of the king when all the wise men, sooth-Sayers, and the magicians had failed.Discovering this magnificent interpretation, the king ordered to bring Yusuf to him. The king was surely impressed by Yusuf after he heard his dream interpretations.When the man was sent to bring Yusuf into kingdom, he denied coming.Yusuf asked," go back and ask your lord (king) why was I casted into the prison, what was I guilty for?

Yusuf also demanded to inquire the matter of the women who cut their hands; indeed my Allah is full of knowledge of their cunning traps. He demanded an inquiry into the matter not because he himself hand any doubt of his confidence, but because was perfectly confident of this and their cunning. Yusuf wanted to inquire the matter into public so that every single person of the kingdom would know that reality behind his imprisonment and they would also know that he was absolutely innocent.

The entire matter reached the king, he came to know that Yusuf wants to enquire the matter to find if he was guilty or not. The king summoned all the women who witnessed the elegance of Yusuf and they knew all how Yusuf was innocent and zulekha insisted him to agree for the evil she wanted.

IV
Chapter

The women who were invited by Zulekha to feast and cut their hands presented before the king. They were questioned about the matter, "What do you know about an incident when you tried to entice Yusuf"?They all cried out in one voice and declared that they had no wrong intentions about Yusuf. With reference to them Zulekha also joined the discourse and accepted her guilt. She said, "Now the truth has come to light, it was I who tried to entice him in fact he is absolutely innocent.

It was the time when the king finally came to know about the entire matter. He discovered that Yusuf is innocent and he was casted into the prison even he had been trapped by the false allegations.With the supreme authority, the king announced, "From now you have an honourable position with us". Yusuf said, "Please place all the resources of the land under my trust for I know how to guard them and I possess the knowledge. Yusuf did not request to king to grant him such powers of the city but he was sure to do justice if the powers are given to him because he possessed such knowledge to serve the capital, he knew the powers of the state would be entertained by someone else the whole state would collapse and the common people of the court and around would suffer during the years of famine.

With this Yusuf was appointed as the governor of the country. There was none other than Yusuf who whom Allah had given the infest knowledge of things. The king, his courtiers, his princes, officers, and men of high ranks recognised his worth had experienced his superiority during the entire decade of his life. He had proved that there was none equal to him in his honesty, righteounous, self-discipline, generosity, intelligence and understanding.

Yusuf knew that there are the hardships going to take place in the country. He though if the measures are not taken the country the areas adjacent to it would also pass through harsh conditions.He wisely took the economic affairs of the country and thought of solving them with the following years of challenge. He was the only one who knew how to guard and utilize the resources of land and could be safely entrusted with them. As soon as he showed his willingness, they heartedly put these affairs in his hands to utilize.

Egypt was the only place in the continent where crops used to grow in abundant amount while the other parts close to it usually fell in the dry and could not grow the maximum resources to feed.Now Yusuf was made the governor of the country, he was given every right to take decisions for the advancement of people, it was all because he was found trust worthy and eligible for it and indeed Allah has given him countless abilities and blessed him with knowledge and wisdom.

By the passage of time the circumstances of Egypt begun to change. The time started with the predictions that Yusuf already had given through interpretation.Seven years passed by when the abundant crops grew and the massive amount of which were stored for the next seven years. With the following preparations of Yusuf all the plans were made which he already had carried to country. Seven years passed and the next seven years of hardships begun to impact the whole county. The whole land of Egypt was under the control of Yusuf now as if it belonged to him and he could claim any piece of it as his and there was no piece of it which could be withheld from him.

Then the seven years of scarcity begun and regime of famine caught up not only Egypt but all over the adjoining countries collectively, accordingly Syria, Palestine, Jordon, and northern part of Arabia begun to suffer from the scarcity of food but besides drought there was some stored food in Egypt because of wise steps taken my Yusuf .Because of the harsh conditions, all those countries decided to bring crops from Egypt and fulfil their needs.The countries had no options except heading towards Egypt and exchange the goods in order to bring crops, like corn, rice and other essentials for survival.

Alike the other countries the people from Palestine also to take crops from Egypt, because Palestine was also the victim of drought and came under the harsh conditions of food.Most caravans started to come from Egypt on the camels, along with these caravans the step brothers of Yusuf too came with these caravans, the brothers who had thrown Yusuf in the dark well. All of ten brothers came without Bin-yamin. As all others caravans who came to Egypt, the brothers of Yusuf also had the same intention of bring corn from the country.

Yusuf used to distribute the yields among the people himself, and his brothers also came into line to collect the food. Yusuf had arranged that no foreign was allowed to barter corn without a special permit from him. Everyone had to present himself before Yusuf for obtaining the special permit for buying a fixed quantity of corn allowed under the famine regulations.

When they appeared in the; line for the food, Yusuf recognised them one by one but they did not even imagine who Yusuf was. His brothers could not recognise Yusuf , when they casted him into the well, he was mere a lad of seventeen and at the time of their meeting, he was grown up man and he had changed his form during this long period, they even could not imagined that the boy who we casted into well is now has become a ruler of Egypt.

They took their needs from the county officials and without recognising Yusuf; they did not recognise Yusuf and Yusuf did not reveal his identity to them, he did not tell them that he was their brother.The country had governed certain rules to distribute the crops in the people. The officials would follow the rules to set by the king.After picking corn from the officials of kingdom, they said, 'we have one more brother in the home that we did not carry him along here, so we want you to give us his share as well'. During the conversation they said, 'we are ten real brothers and one step who is from the same father but from the second mother.

Discovering the matter, Yusuf came to know they he was not wrong in identifying them. He came to know that he is Binyamin who they talked about.Yusuf agreed and said, "Well, your brothers share is also available to be provided, next time bring your brother along with you so we can ensure them too with his hare.Yusuf ensured him about the rule of the government that his share can't be provided in his absence they must take him along to collect his share as well."Bring your step brother to me, don't you see I give full measure and I the best of hosts"? Said Yusuf."If you fail to bring you brother to me then you will be denied to take any share from here, you will not be allowed to enter the country", Yusuf added.

Along with this Yusuf tried to win them over by reminding them of his liberal and generous treatment with them, because he yearned to know how his family had fared during his absence.Listening to Yusuf, they said that they will convince their father to take him along and we will do our best to bring him along with us when we come again to Egypt.

The step brothers of Yusuf also had carried some goods to barter the corn as other people from countries around. It was the system by which people exchanged their goods to collect corn and other eatable for Egypt.it was the time when people used to bargain things while exchanging the things with each other, there was some defined currency for buying goods.

Yusuf ordered his slaves, "place secretly in their saddle bags the goods they have bartered for corn. Yusuf did this because he wanted to make them feel comfortable and it was the kind of invitations to come again to collect grains.

V
Chapter

The events of the several years after his coming into power have been left out but out of the sake of brevity,The time when all the step brothers of Yusuf returned back to Palestine (kanan) from Egypt. They carried loads of corn on their camels as other caravans of the countries.

Reaching home they said to their father, " dear Abba, the corn has henceforth been denied to us, the king told to bring your step brother along with you so we will be able to bring his share of corn as well'. They explained how the king has constrained their brother's share and ordered to bring him along next time to collect his share.They told father to send their brother (Binyamin) with them to fetch corn and they will take full responsibility of him. In response to these lines, Yaqub replied, "should I entrust him to you as I entrusted his brother to you before"?

Only Allah is the supreme protector and he is the only merciful. By this Yaqub expressed his inner feelings about their step brother and he now only can trust Allah not the sons any more. Yaqub was already grieved by the separation of Yusuf so he could not think of let their sons take Bin-yamin from him like they had taken away Yusuf years before.

When they opened their bags, they found their merchandise had been returned to them. All their goods had been put in their bags in which they carried the corn from Egypt. Seeing this they cried with joy, dear Abba , " look here what else we desire? Here are our goods returned to us. We will go back and bring provisions and food for our family; we will take good care of our brother and bring extra camel of corn".

The merchandise they founded in their bags which Yusuf had placed back made them gratified and pleased; it made them happy to go back to Egypt to bring more loads of corn for their family.By watching this Yaqub replied, "I will never send him with you until you give me a pledge in Allah's name that you shall bring him back to me unless it is that you are rendered helpless by circumstances".

When they gave their solemn pledges, on that he said, "Note well that Allah is guarding and watching over this pledge of ours".Yaqub was not willing to send bin-yamin with his step brothers; it was troubling Yaqub as Yusuf was sent with them.

As Yusuf, Yaqub finally agreed to send bin-yamin with them to fetch corn from Egypt. Yaqub lectured to their sons, "do not enter the capital of Egypt from the one gate but go into it by different gates". "However know it well, I can't protect you from Allah, he has any authority what so ever, he added. He advised them to be on their guard against the dangerous political situations in the capital, Yuqub did not want his sons should be captured and blamed to be the thieves, he advised tem to be safe in the country without violating in social and political rules. By these lines it seemed that Yaqub was so careful for all of them, so he gave them instructions to follow while entering the city.

It happened, they entered the capital by different gates as their father had advised them, but the precautionary measure proved ineffective against Allah's will Yaqub was not able to hold the balance between trust in Allah and adoption of precautionary measures. Yaqub has done his best to avoid the fear the he had in his heart, Yaqub advised by the knowledge that Allah has given him.

He admonished them for their ill treatment with their brother Yusuf so that they should not dare repeat it in case of Binyamin.Entering the country, they presented themselves before Yusuf. When Yusuf saw that they had also carried his brother (bin-yamin) with them. He called Binyamin alone himself and said secretly, "I am your brother Yusuf, who was lost. Their reunion after a separation of twenty years turned into consolation. Yusuf consoled his brother and said, "You need not to worry now, surely our brothers offended us, but the time has gone, there is an ease now".

While arranging the loading of packs Yusuf's brothers, Yusuf himself put his cup in the bag of his own Bin-Yamin. He did it with his knowledge and consent. The cup was made of gold in which the king used to drink.After when the brothers where ready to return back, the officials or slaves of the kingdom shouted," O cameleers, you are thieves!Turning back they asked, "What is it that you are missing?The royal servants replied, "We do not find the cup of the king". But Yusuf knew the cup was inside the bag of his brother, Bin-yamin.The head man of the royal slaves announced, "The one who will restore it, will be awarded a camel load of corn".

The brothers replied, "We swear by Allah, you know well that we have not come to this country for creating any trouble and we are not thieves"."We are the victims of drought you know it well and we come here only for corn to eat but we are not thieves", they added these words so politely."What would be the punishments, if you found to be the liars", royal slaves questioned,"The punishment will be himself made the bondsman, if the cup is found in his bag, at home we punish such offenders like this," brothers replied.Both the royal slaves and the brothers agreed to check their bags and the punishment will be given to one who will be found thief.

The royal servants started to search their bags; they began to check the bags of his step brothers before searching the bag of his own brother.At last Yusuf took out the cup from his real brother's bag. They found the cup inside Binyamin's bag, but Yusuf did not use the word thief for his brother, for he was not really a thief.At this discovery when all step brothers found the cup in Bin-yamin's bag they said, "There is nothing strange in it that he theft as his brother Yusuf theft before him."

The brothers really did believe that Bin-yamin had engaged in theft.By hearing these words Yusuf suppressed his feelings and did not reveal the secret over them but said this in under tune, what bad people you are! You are accusing me on my face, indeed Allah knows the best.

I was now clear to keep bin-yamin there because the cup was found in his bag, Yusuf desired to free his brother from the oppression of his cruel brothers and Bin-yamin himself was reluctant to go back with their father. The brothers said, "O glorious sir, he has a very old father, take one of us in his stead, we see that you are very generous man".

Knowing about their father, Yusuf understood that talked about his father Yaqub how he had turned an old man and lost his vision.The situation went extremely rigid for all those brothers , their father had already lost faith in them in regard to Yusuf and this time that had taken pledge to take care of bin-Yamin and take him back home. They were worried to go back without bin-yamin and what pretext they would keep this time before their father. They tried to convince Yusuf to keep one of them instead of bin-yamim.

"Allah forbid us that we should seize someone else other than one with whom we have found our property" replied Yusuf.They failed to convince Yusuf to seize one of them instead of Bin-Yamin and went into a corner and conferred together. The oldest of them said, "You know that your father had taken solemn pledge from you in the name of Allah, you also know you have also wronged Yusuf before this, I will not leave this land until my father gives me permission or Allah decides in my favour. Go back home and tell your father that your son had theft and we did not see him stealing it, we are stating what we saw, tell the caravan that we came with and people who met us during the way".

Now Bin-yamin and his step brother, Yuhda both stayed with Yusuf and all other brothers went back to Palestine to narrate the entire story to their father.

VI
Chapter

Heading back to home, Kanan, they explained everything to their father what was being done with Bin-yamin. They narrated all what happened in Egypt and especially with Bin-Yamin.Hearing this, Yaqub said, "your souls have made another thing easy for you, well, I will bear this too with grace, maybe Allah will bring all them to me for he knows everything and his works are based on wisdom".

Yaqub repeated the same words those he had said when his sons took Yusuf away and rumoured that Yusuf was eaten by wolf and brought his shirt with false blood. Now they came with making bin-yamin the thief, both the pretexts were so easy for them to represent to their father.The event resembled the past when Yusuf was taken by them along and came with meagre excuse, this time they came with same attitude which proved them to be the weird creations. It was the time when Yaqub was passed two more decades and he had attained an old age so the separation of his son was too hard to bear.

Yaqub was already bothered about the separation of Yusuf, now he consoled himself with patience to bear the pain of Bin-yamin and Yahuda who denied coming back from Egypt. Bin-yamin's separation renewed the aching of Yusuf in Yaqub. Yahuda did not come back to home because he was the eldest and he knew that what they had done with Yusuf who had grieve their father so much , this time he did not returned to home his father his face with disgrace , he preferred to remain with Bin-yamin and somehow compensated for their wrong doings.

Then Yaqub turned his face from them and cried, "Alas for Yusuf!He was sorely oppressed with suppressed sorrow and his eyes had become white with grief. He remembered the dream of Yusuf when he first time advised Yusuf not to reveal his dream to anyone.

All the sons grew serious and they understood that their father had deeply grieved by the pain of Yusuf and Bin-yamin. They responded and exclaimed, "By Allah! You have not ceased to think about Yusuf and now things have come to such a pass that you will ruin your heath or yourself with grief for him".

He answered, "I complaint to Allah alone of my sorrow and grief. And I know from Allah hat you do not know, my children go and search for Yusuf, don't despair of Allah's mercy, it is that the unbelievers who despair of his mercy'. "You readily believed that my son, whom I know to be a noble character had committed the theft of a cup, you have behaved in his case just as you behaved in the case of his elder brother. You made away with him and then pretended without any pangs of conscience that a wolf had devoured him and now with the same ease you tell me that other brother has committed a theft" Yaqub added.

Things changed, the agony of Yaqub crossed the demarcations in canon and Yusuf with his brother in Egypt also longed for their father too. The separation of fathers and the sons yearned to meet and end up the prolonged pain and suffering of all those past years which they passed with patience and did not complaint for a single moment.

Because of despair and grief Yaqub was saddened for his son's loss but he had firm believe that Yusuf was alive, it was the consolation by Allah that he never had lost his hope even with the darkest shadows of despair and agony. He therefore insisted his sons to find out Yusuf and Bin-yamin to bring them back to him.

For bringing back Bin-yamin the brothers had no other option to stay home in Kanan but they were asked to leave their home again for corn and good news of their brothers.Once again all the brothers went to Egypt, entering the royal kingdom of Yusuf they said, " dear exalted sir, we and our family are in great distress , we have be able to bring only goods of scant for barter, we request you to give us full measure of grain, and be charitable to us.it will be charitable if you give us much grain as we required to fulfil our needs because the goods we have brought for its barter are less value than of the grain we required".

They begged Yusuf to help them whatever he can grant with. This time they had come with merge to barter, the drought had surely put them in harsh conditions. They narrated everything which had been going on in their home with their family; they explained how they were facing the hardships and came without any solid resource to bring corn once again from Yusuf.

The attitude they adopted was well-intentioned and smelly, after begging Yusuf to be generous towards them, they recalled Allah and the fact he will reward those who give generously, this was the absolute indication of their hypocritical behaviour, because despite living in the way that is contrary to religion and the good pleasure of Allah and their forgetting Allah during the course of their actions, they recalled him when their interests were at stake. At this, yusuf could not contain himself no longer, he exclaimed, "Do you know what you did with yusuf and his brother, when you were ignorant?It surprised them and they cried out why?They were surprised knowing the question asked by Yusuf about himself and his brother Bin-yamin. They lost in wonder and recalled their past actions they had done which put them into bewilderment.

'Are you indeed yusuf' they asked.He replied, "Yes, I am Yusuf, and here is my brother.Hearing this they said' "by Allah, Allah has exalted you above us, we have been indeed sinful'. They managed to surmise that they were dealing with Yusuf, declaring their regret and the fact they had committed an error. They accepted that Allah had signed Yusuf and that he had chosen over them.

Despite that fact that Yusuf was in position to have punished or treated his brothers badly, he did not question them rather he did not condemn them.

Yusuf replied, "Today, no penalty shall be inflicted on you, may Allah forgive you! Go home take this shirt of mine and cast this over the face of my father and he shall recover his sight, then bring all the family members of your family to me'. He asked Allah for forgiveness for them, reminding them that Allah is the most merciful. This behaviour of Yusuf was an ample to all the faithful, ignorant people are inspired by hatred in such situations.

Now Yusuf directed their brothers to return back home, he offered them his shirt to rub on Yaqub's face and asked them to bring the entire family to him. Because of the grief of Yusuf , his father had lost his eye sight therefore Yusuf directed their brothers to caste his shirt on the eyes of

Yaqub and he would get back his vision.

VII
Chapter

The caravan of brothers begun to travel from Egypt, they carried the shirt of Yusuf along with them that Yusuf gave to them for curing his father's sight. There were miles to go, and the caravan was eight days afar from kanan (pasetine) but Yaqub smelt the fragrance of Yusuf. For all these years of separation Yaqub never smelt this fragrance even his eyes turned white in cry but this time he smelt the fragrance of Yusuf which was obviously from Allah. Even Yaqub acknowledged to his family that I am smelling the fragrance of beloved Yusuf. He never claimed such things during the years of separation but once the caravan left Egypt he revealed the secret which seemed to joke to his family.

Yaqub knew that Yusuf is alive and he was sure that he will meet him again, for which his family said, "You are dived into your old elusions. His family was not ready to accept his insights; they considered him the blind believer of his old thoughts and elusions. They used to speak hard words to Yaqub and tried to make him forget everything about Yusuf which could not work for any end and they failed to eliminate Yaqub's love for Yusuf. Since they could not understand the acquaintance of prophets, they were unaware about their revelations that Allah sent them. Yaqub kept waiting firmly his heart was content and he had won the greatest patience.

After the days or a week ,the caravan reached home , the bearer casted the shirt of Yusuf on Yaqub's face, after casting the shirt on his face , his sight recovered and he said, " did not I tell you that I know the things form Allah that you don't know. A few days before I told you that I smelt the fragrance of Yusuf" he said.

The brothers of Yusuf felt that they were guilty for what they did with Yusuf , even they accepted their actions of bad deeds they had done the years before , for which Yusuf had Yaqub lived years in separation and pain but Neither Yusuf nor Yaqub took revenge of their guilt they instead Allah forgiveness from Allah for them.

All the brothers altogether exclaimed to their father and asked for their forgiveness. After some Yaqoob and all the sons went back to Egypt to meet Yusuf. When the entire caravan reached the kingdom and Yaqoob saw his Yusuf alive there was joy and happiness all around.

Yusuf received his father and his brother with great honour and respect.Yusuf seated his father on the throne along with him and all the step brothers bowed before Yusuf , both Yusuf and Yaqoob witnessed the scene and Yusuf directed towards them and said, Abba this the dream that I had dreamed of my childhood and I came to you for the interpretation , today Allah fulfilled the dream and showed us the dream with reality.